This book has been donated to
The Concord Library in the honor of

Steve Richard

this _16_ day of _Dec._, 201_6_ _Dan Fisher_
President

ROTARY
SERVING
HUMANITY

Rotary
Club of Concord

BUDDY
FOR
PRESIDENT

Hans Wilhelm

HARPER
An Imprint of HarperCollinsPublishers

My name is Hunter Green and this is my dog, Buddy. Buddy is the best dog in the whole world. That's why I want him to become our next president. What? You think dogs can't become president? Well, then it's time to change that. IT'S TIME FOR BUDDY!

Let me tell you why Buddy is so special:

He's always happy to see me—even if I
have been gone for less than thirty seconds.

Buddy helps me with the chores.

He makes taking a bath an adventure!

Buddy has everything you'd want in a great president:

He loves the great outdoors (just like President Theodore Roosevelt).

He believes in sharing and helping others (just like President Franklin D. Roosevelt).

He is a born leader who is an awesome
saxophone player (just like President Bill Clinton).

Nobody knows how to kiss babies better than
Buddy. He'll slobber himself into everybody's heart.

Who could better "preserve, protect, and defend the Constitution of the United States" than a hound? I'll tell you: No one!

When Buddy is president, other dogs will want to be in politics too. Washington will never be the same again!

Buddy will be our top dog! He will put his
presidential paw print only on good laws, like bedtime
just for grown-ups and more playtime for kids!

Everybody will cheer when Buddy
introduces a law so that all kids must have
a safe place to live with grown-ups and dogs
who love them with all their hearts.

Kids will read more! Reading becomes real fun when you have someone to read to. Dogs are the best listeners.

Now dogs will be allowed to teach. And their classes will be very different.

On the chalkboard:
Play nice
take naps
lick a face
hug and
snuggle

FETCH
BEG
HEEL
JUMP
SIT
ROLL OVE
LIE D
COME

You can take a class on how to chew up a stinky sneaker in one sitting.

Recess will become the most important class.
(I hope this alone will make you vote for Buddy.)

President Buddy will make sure that cars, school buses, planes, and trains have no roofs. Fresh air for everyone!

WILD DOGS AIRWAY

NEW NATIONAL ANTHEM

("Take Me Out to the Ball Game" translated into Caninese)

Woof, woof, woof, woof, woof, woof, woof,
Woof, woof, woof, woof, woof, woof.
Woof, woof, woof, woof, woof, woof, woof, woof, woof,
Woof, woof, woof, woof, woof, woof, woof, woof, woof.
Woof, woof, woof, woof, woof, woof, woof, woof, woof,
Woof, woof, woof, woof, woof, woof, woof.
Woof, woof, woof, woof, woof, woof, woof, woof,
Woof, woof, woof, woof, woof.

We will have to change the national anthem so that *everybody* can sing it.

Of course, other countries will be very jealous of Buddy, so they will also elect dogs as their leaders. The whole world is going to the dogs!

Once a year all leaders will come together for a
summit and play ball on the White House lawn.

Buddy will bring dogs and people together like no president has before.

All the leaders in the world will be best
friends with Buddy. Their tails will wag with
delight when they hear his voice.

No country will need an army anymore.
Dogs have no time for that. Instead of bombs
and bullets, they will throw Frisbees or learn
how to dance the conga.

Dogs will rule the world! Buddy will be the
best president ever! Now it is up to you. When
Election Day comes, make sure you vote for Buddy.
Because if you don't vote for him . . .

. . . the other guy will win.

ISBN 978-0-06-240366-7 (trade bdg.)

The artist used watercolor to create the illustrations for this book.
Typography by Rachel Zegar
16 17 18 19 20   SCP   10 9 8 7 6 5 4 3 2 1
❖
First Edition